Enna Hittims

by

Diana Wynne Jones

Illustrated by Peter Utton

You do not need to read this page –
just get on with the book!

First published in 2006 in Great Britain by
Barrington Stoke Ltd
www.barringtonstoke.co.uk

ISBN-10: 1-842993-96-8
ISBN-13: 978-1-84299-396-5

Printed in Great Britain by Bell & Bain Ltd

MEET THE AUTHOR – DIANA WYNNE JONES

What is your favourite animal?
Cats, but I like dogs too
What is your favourite boy's name?
John
What is your favourite girl's name?
Angharad
What is your favourite food?
Potatoes in all forms – chips, mash, crisps, saute, jacket, roast – yum!
What is your favourite music?
Anything played on a cello
What is your favourite hobby?
Writing

MEET THE ILLUSTRATOR – PETER UTTON

What is your favourite animal?
Cat
What is your favourite boy's name?
Henry
What is your favourite girl's name?
Fifi
What is your favourite food?
Biscuits
What is your favourite hobby?
Writing

To Johnny,
because I couldn't write the cats just yet

Contents

Chapter 1
Mumps

Anne Smith hated having mumps. She had to miss two school outings. Her face came up so fat and purple that both her parents laughed at her when they were at home. But she was left alone rather a lot, because her parents couldn't afford to take time off from their jobs.

The first day was terrible. Anne's temperature went up and up, and the higher it got, the more and more hungry she became. By the time her father got off work early and came home, she was starving.

"But people don't get hungry with a temperature!" Mr Smith said, grinning as he looked at Anne's great purple face.

"I don't care. I want five sausages and two helpings of chips and lots of ketchup," said Anne. "Quick or I'll die!"

So Mr Smith raced out to the chip shop. But when he came back, Anne couldn't open her mouth to bite the sausage. She couldn't chew the chips. And the ketchup stung the inside of her mouth. It felt as if she was eating nettles.

"I told you so," said Mr Smith.

Anne didn't lose her temper often but now she burst into tears and threw all the food on the floor. "I'm so hungry!" she yelled. "It's torture!"

Of course, it hurt to shout, too.

Mr Smith didn't often get cross. But now he had to clean ketchup off the carpet. He lost his temper and shouted, "Do that again, and I'll spank you, mumps or not!"

"I hate you," said Anne. "I hate everything." And she sat and sulked. When you've got mumps, there's not much else you can do.

"I think she's got grumps as well as mumps," Mrs Smith said when she got in from work.

It did seem to be so. For the next few days, nothing made Anne happy. She tried walking slowly round the house looking for things to do. Nothing seemed interesting and her face hurt. She tried playing with Tibby, the cat, but Tibby was boring. She tried watching DVDs. Some were boring and some made her laugh, but that was even worse. Laughing hurt. She tried reading, but that was the same, and her fat, swollen chin kept getting in the way. Everything was boring.

Mrs Harvey next door was very kind. She came in to get Anne some lunch. But Mrs Harvey didn't understand that crusty pizza and an orange are the last things you want to eat when you've got mumps.

Anne told her parents all this when they got home. The result was that her parents stopped saying, "It's the way you feel with mumps." Instead, they said, "Oh for heaven's sake, Anne, do stop grumbling!" every time Anne opened her mouth.

Anne took herself and her great purple face back to bed. She lay still and stared at the shape her legs made under the duvet. She hated her parents. *I'm so ill*, she thought, *and no one cares!*

The next minute she had invented Enna Hittims.

Chapter 2
Enna

It all happened in a flash. When she thought about it later, Anne thought it must have been because her legs under the duvet made a shape like a landscape with two long hills and a green jungly valley in between. There was a long fold in the duvet running down from her left foot and it looked like a gorge, a deep valley, where a river might run. Even though Anne felt cross and fed up, she began to think what it would be like if you were very small and could explore those hills and that valley.

Enna Hittims was very small. The name Enna Hittims was Anne Smith backwards. But there's no way you can say "Htims." You have to put a noise in between the H and the t, so that made Enna's second name into Hittims. It was just the right name for her. She was a bold and brave lady – a real hero, even if she was just four centimetres tall. She was tall and slim and strong. Her dark black hair was cut short and her face was thin and brown. There was no sign of mumps in Enna Hittims, and she was scared of nothing. Enna Hittims was born to explore and have adventures.

Enna Hittims started life on her parents' farm beside the Fold River, just below Left Toe Mountain. She was working in their cornfield one day, when she dug up an old sword. Enna Hittims picked it up and swished it, and it cut through the spade. It was a magic sword that could cut through anything. Enna Hittims took the sword home. Her parents were lazing about and Enna cut the kitchen table in half to show them what the sword could do.

"I'm leaving," she said. "I want to have adventures."

"No, you're not," said her parents. "We won't allow it. We need you to do all the work."

Then Enna Hittims saw that all her parents wanted her for was to work for them. She cut both their heads off with the magic sword and set off from the farm. She took only a small parcel of food. She'd have to look for what she might find.

In this way Enna Hittims began the most exciting and interesting kind of life.

Chapter 3
Heroes

For the next few days Anne could only think about Enna Hittims and her adventures. She lay in bed and looked at the landscape the duvet made and thought about what might happen to Enna Hittims in it.

The first brave thing Enna Hittims did was to kill a tiger at Ankle Bend. Tibby put this idea into Anne's head when she came to sleep on her bed. After that Enna Hittims climbed up Left Toe Mountain. The landscape there was even more wondrous.

In the giant fern forest near the top of
the mountain, where monkeys chattered and
parrots screamed, Enna Hittims met two
more brave explorers, who were about to be
killed by a savage gorilla. Enna Hittims cut
the gorilla's head off for them, and the two
explorers became her loyal friends. Their
names were Marlene and Spike. The heroic
three set off to find the treasure that was
guarded by the dragon on Knee Cliffs.

By this time, Anne was finding Enna
Hittims and her friends so interesting that
she just had to get out of bed for her drawing
book and felt tips and draw pictures of their
adventures. Of course, when she got back into
bed, the landscape had changed. The green
patch, which had been the fern forest, had
got down between Anne's feet and become
the Caves of Emerald, and the Fold River had
turned into Toagra Falls.

Enna and her friends understood that the land they were exploring was magic and changed all the time so they weren't scared. The landscape changed each time Anne got in and out of bed. They soon worked out that a powerful magician was trying to stop them getting the dragon's treasure. Enna promised to finish off the magician when they had killed the dragon.

The three friends explored all over the duvet. Anne made drawing after drawing of them. She didn't mind Tibby being so boring. When Tibby was curled up asleep on the bed, she stayed still for Anne to draw her. Anne meant Tibby to be the dragon in the end, but until then, Tibby made a good model for all the other monsters the three heroes killed. For the human monsters, Anne found photos of her parents and her cousins. Then she copied the photos but added glaring eyes and long teeth.

Enna was easy to draw. Her bold dark face gave Anne no trouble at all. Marlene was almost as easy, because she was the opposite of her friend. Marlene was fair and small and not very brave. Enna often had to snap at Marlene for being so scared. Spike was more trouble to draw. Of course he had spiky hair, but his name really came from the magic spike he used as his weapon. He was small and quick, with a squashed up face. At first, Anne kept drawing him looking like a monkey. Then she got good at drawing him.

She drew and drew. Every time she got out of bed and the landscape changed, she thought of new adventures. Anne didn't notice Mrs Harvey come in with her lunch. She didn't notice if her parents were in or out. She didn't notice anything.

"Thank goodness!" said Mr and Mrs Smith.

And then disaster struck. Just before lunchtime when Anne was all alone in the house, every one of her felt tips ran out.

"Oh bother!" Anne wailed, almost in tears. She scribbled angrily, but even the purple felt tip only made a pale, squeaky line. It was awful. Enna and her friends were in the middle of meeting the hermit who knew where to find the dragon. Anne was dying to draw the hermit's cave. Enna was holding the edge of her magic sword to the foolish hermit's throat. Anne had a photo of Mr Smith all ready to copy to be the hermit. She was looking forward to giving him long hair and a scraggly beard and a look of utter terror.

"Oh, bother!" Anne shouted, and threw the felt tips across the room.

Tibby by now knew all about Anne in this mood. She jumped off Anne's bed and galloped for the door. Mrs Harvey came in with Anne's lunch just then. Tibby slipped around Mrs Harvey and ran away.

"Here you are, dear," Mrs Harvey said, puffing rather, "Those stairs are hard work." She put a tray down on Anne's knees. "I've done you macaroni cheese and some nice stewed apple. You can eat that, can't you?"

Anne knew Mrs Harvey was being kind. She smiled, in spite of being so cross and said, "Yes, thank you."

"I should think you'd be well enough to go downstairs a bit now," Mrs Harvey said. Then she went away again.

Chapter 4
Giant

Anne sighed and looked back at the duvet.
To her surprise, Enna Hittims had killed the
hermit while Anne was talking to Mrs
Harvey. Anne had meant the hermit to stay
alive and show the heroes the way to the
dragon. She stared at Enna Hittims who was
coolly wiping her magic sword clean on a
handy corner of the duvet. "Sorry if I lost my
temper," Enna Hittims was saying, "but I
don't think the old fool knew a thing about
that dragon."

Anne was rather shocked. She hadn't known that Enna Hittims was that unfeeling.

"You did quite right," said Spike. "You know I'm beginning to think that dragon may not exist at all."

"Me, too," answered Enna. She hitched her sword to her belt rather grimly. "And if someone is having us on ..."

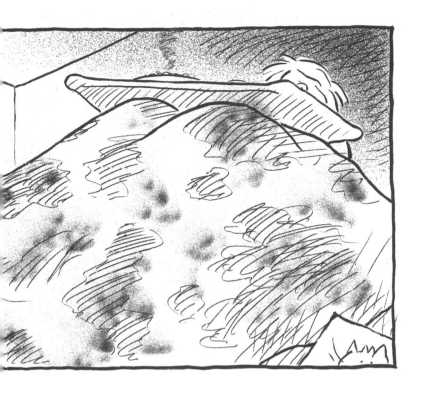

"Enna," Marlene said, "the landscape's changed again. Over there."

The three heroes swung around and shaded their eyes with their hands to look at the tray across Anne's lap. "You're right!" said Enna Hittims. "Well done, Marlene! What is it up there?"

"A tableland," said Spike. "There are two white mountains, and one has steam coming from it. Do you think it could be the dragon?"

"Probably only a new volcano," said Enna Hittims. "Let's go and see."

The three heroes set off along the top of Anne's right leg. They walked quickly in single file, and Anne watched them in some alarm. She did not want them climbing over her lunch while she tried to eat it.

"Go back," she said. "The dragon's going to be down by my right knee."

"What was that?" Marlene whispered in a nervous way as she followed the other two up the slant of Anne's leg.

"Just thunder. We're always hearing it," said Enna. "Don't whinge, Marlene."

The three heroes stood in a row with their chins on the edge of the lunch tray.

"Well how about that!" said Enna. She pointed to the plate of macaroni cheese. "That hill of hot pipes – do you think it's a factory of some kind?"

"There could be a baby dragon in each pipe," Marlene said.

"What are those shiny things?" asked Spike and he pointed at the knife, fork and spoon.

"Silver bars," Enna said. "We'll have to find an elephant and tow them away. This must be the dragon's lair. But what's that?"

The three heroes stared at the bowl of stewed apple.

"Pale yellow slush," said Spike, "with a sour smell. Is it dragon sick?"

"It could be some kind of melted gold," Marlene said. She looked across the tray slowly, searching for some clue. Her eyes

went on, up the hill of Anne's body. She jumped and grabbed Spike's sleeve. "Look!" she whispered. "Up there!"

Spike looked. He turned to Enna. "Look up, but do it slowly so no one sees," he murmured. "Isn't that a giant face up there?"

Enna glanced up. She nodded. "Right. Very big and purple, with little, piggy eyes. It's some kind of giant. We'll have to kill it."

"Now look here ..." Anne called out.

But the three heroes took her voice for thunder, just as they always did. Enna went on briskly making her plans.

"Marlene and Spike, you go around the tableland, one on each side, and climb up its hair. Swing over when you're above the nose and stab an eye each. I'll go in over the middle and see if I can cut its fat throat."

Spike and Marlene nodded and raced away around the edges of the tray.

Anne did not wait to see if the plan worked. She picked up the tray and pushed it on top of her bedside table. Then she scrambled out of bed as fast as she could go. This of course changed the landscape again. All three heroes toppled over and fell under the duvet.

Anne hoped that had finished them off. It should have done. After all, she had made them all up.

Chapter 5
Escape

To give them time to die, or vanish, or something, Anne went down to the kitchen and got herself a glass of milk. She looked for Tibby to give her some milk, too, but Tibby had gone out through her cat flap. Anne went back to her bedroom. She hoped the heroes had gone.

They were still there. Spike was up on her pillow. He was whirling his spike around his head on the end of a rope. He let it go just as Anne came in, and it flew across the bed and stuck firmly into the edge of the tray. It was a tin tray, but the spike was magic, of course, and would stick to anything Spike wanted it to. Spike, Enna and Marlene all took hold of the rope and pulled. The tray slid. It tipped.

"No, stop!" Anne said weakly. She knew the tray was half off the table already.

One end of the tray came down into the bed. Down slid the macaroni cheese, and down slid the stewed apple after it. The heroes saw it coming. They jumped expertly for safety, up onto the pillows. They were used to this kind of thing. While Anne was still staring at macaroni and apple as it dripped onto her sheets, Spike dashed down and took his spike back.

Enna Hittims walked around the marsh of stewed apple. She cut a macaroni tube in half with her sword. "It's not alive," she said. "Don't just stand there, Marlene. We're going up that ramp to find that giant and finish him off. I can see it's the giant that's been

changing the landscape all the time. No giant's going to do that to me!"

They started scrambling up the tray. Anne hoped it would be too slippery for them. But no. Spike used his spike to help them scramble up. Enna used her sword and hacked steps into the metal. She walked up the tray backwards, dragging Marlene with her other hand. She kept snapping, "Do come on, Marlene!"

Even before they were half-way up to the table, Anne knew that the only thing to do was to pick the tray up and tip them back into the stewed apple. And then put the tray on top of them and press. But she couldn't bring herself to do anything so nasty. She stood and watched them climb on top of the bedside table. Enna stood with her hands on her hips and looked out across Anne's bedroom.

"We're in the giant's house now," she said as if she knew all about it.

"And he'll be a mountain of cat food before long," said Spike. Marlene laughed.

Anne ran out of the bedroom and shut the door with a slam. She ran down to the living room and stood with her hands together and her eyes shut. "Go away, all three of you!" she prayed. "Go. Disappear. Vanish. You're only made up!"

Then she went back upstairs to see if the prayer had worked. Her bedroom door was still shut, but there was some kind of purple tube sticking out from under the door. As Anne bent down to see what it was, she heard Enna's voice from behind the door. "Well, what is out there Marlene?"

"A huge passage," Marlene's voice answered. The tube was the purple felt tip with its inside taken out. It swung sideways as Anne looked.

"Oh!" said Marlene. "There's a giant out there now! I can see its toes."

"Great!" said Enna. "Let's get after it."

There was a burring, splintering noise. The tip of Enna's sword, together with a lot of sawdust, made a neat half circle in the bottom of the bedroom door.

Chapter 6
Downstairs

Anne ran away to the bathroom and sat on the edge of the bath, thinking what to do. She heard the voices of the three heroes out on the landing. She shut the bathroom door, very softly. Nothing happened. After a while she felt she had better go and see what the heroes were doing.

There was a hole like a mouse hole in the bottom of her bedroom door. The heroes were on their way downstairs. Anne could hear

Enna saying, "Come on Marlene! Just let yourself drop and Spike will catch you." They seemed to be half-way down.

Anne crept out to see how they were getting downstairs. They were letting themselves down on the rope tied to Spike's magic spike. Marlene was dangling and spinning on the rope. To Anne's surprise, she was wearing a new dress of a pretty bluebell colour.

"Ooh. It's so high!" she said.

"Don't be such a wimp!" said Enna. "We're half-way down."

Spike was keeping guard. "There's a giant on the stairs above us," he whispered.

Enna glanced up at Anne. "You two go on," she said. "It's only a small one. You two get down and look for the big giants, while I slice a few of this one's toes off to keep it busy."

Anne had to run back to the bathroom again. She didn't want to lose her toes. Then she remembered that her bedroom would be safe now and went back there.

It was the most awful mess, even if you didn't count the lunch in the bed. The heroes had pulled books and jigsaws and games out of the shelves. Enna had slashed Anne's piggy bank to bits with her sword and cut up the money inside. Spike had pulled out all Anne's CDs. She could see the scratches his spike had made, right across her favourite ones. Someone had put stewed apple footprints all over Anne's drawings. But it was Marlene who had done the most damage. She had cut a ragged circle out of Anne's best sweatshirt to make herself a new dress.

This made Anne so angry that she almost ran downstairs. By now she hated all three heroes. Enna Hittims was bossy and bloodthirsty. Spike was a vandal. And Marlene was so awful that she deserved the way Enna ordered her about!

Anne wished she had never made them up. But she could see now that she wasn't going to be rid of them by just wishing. She was going to have to do something, however nasty that might be.

As she arrived at the bottom of the stairs, shaking but sure of herself, there was a ringing SMASH! from the living room and the sound of tiny bits of china pattering on the carpet. Anne knew it was her mum's best lamp.

The heroes came scampering around the living room door into the hall. "Too many hazards in there," Enna said. "Now let's see. We're sure the small purple-faced giant is only a servant left on guard. Where can we go to kill the big ones when they come back?"

"The kitchen," said Spike. "They'll want to eat."

"Us, probably," Marlene quavered.

"Don't moan, Marlene," said Enna. "Right. To the kitchen!" She held her sword up and led the other two at a run around the open kitchen door.

Something in the kitchen went ching-BOING! And there was the glop-glop-glop as something spilt out of a bottle. "Oh no!" said Anne. She had left the milk bottle on the floor while she was looking for Tibby. Worse still, she remembered the way Tibby always knew when there was milk on the floor. She could not let Tibby get in the way of the magic sword. She ran across the hall.

"My new dress is soaked!" she heard Marlene wail. Then came the sound of Tibby's cat flap opening. Marlene gasped, "A monster!"

"What a splendid one!" Enna cried out. "You two guard my rear while I kill it."

Chapter 7
Out!

By the time Anne got to the kitchen, Enna was standing, ready for battle, in front of Tibby, blocking Tibby's way to the pool of milk on the floor. And Tibby, who had no idea about magic swords, was crouched down. Her tail was swishing to and fro and she was staring greedily at Enna. Anne could see Tibby thought Enna was a new kind of mouse.

Anne charged through the kitchen and caught Tibby just as she pounced. "Oh-ho!" shouted Enna Hittims. The magic sword

swung at Anne's right foot. Spike sprang at Anne's left foot and stabbed. Tibby struggled and clawed. But Anne hung on to Tibby. She ran out in to the hall, kicking the kitchen door shut behind her, and did not let go of Tibby until the door was shut. Then she dropped Tibby. Tibby stood all ruffled and cross. She gave Anne the look that meant they would not be on speaking terms for some time. Then she stalked away upstairs.

Anne sat on the bottom stair. She watched the blood ooze from a round hole in her left toe and more blood trickle from a deep cut on her right ankle. "How lucky I didn't invent them poisoned weapons!" she said.

She sat and thought. Surely she could defeat these three tiny heroes, if she went about it the right way. She needed armour really.

Anne went up to her bedroom. Tibby was now crouched on Anne's bed. She was picking pieces of macaroni cheese out of the stewed apple. Tibby loved cheese. She looked up at Anne with the look that meant, "Stop me if you dare!"

"You eat it," said Anne. "Be my guest. Stuff yourself. It'll keep you up here out of danger." She got dressed. She put on her thickest jeans and jumper and her black school shoes. Then she put on the zip-up plastic jacket too to make sure. She tied the covers of her drawing book around her legs to make even more sure. Then she collected a handful of shoelaces, string, and belts and picked up the tray. It had little regular cuts in it where Enna had carved her steps. Mrs Harvey wouldn't be pleased.

Anne shut her bedroom door to keep Tibby in there and went down to the living room. She stepped over the bits of the china lamp to the dining area and fetched out the tea trolley.

Then she spent a long time tying the tray to the front of the trolley. She tested it, and tried it again. When she had it tied firmly, so that the tray mowed along the carpet as the trolley was pushed, and nothing could get under the bottom edge of the tray, Anne picked up an umbrella. She was ready.

She pushed the trolley out into the hall. She lay on her tummy across the top of the trolley and turned the handle of the kitchen door. She opened the door as softly as she could. She peeped inside.

She was in luck. The three heroes thought they had defeated her. They were relaxing and filling their waterskins at the edge of the pool of milk. "Now remember to go for the big giants' eyes," Enna Hittims was saying. "You can hold on to their ears if they have short hair."

"No, you can't!" Anne shouted. She shoved off with one foot and sent the trolley through the pool of milk towards them. The tray pushed a tidal wave of milk in front of it as it went. The heroes had to leap back and run, or they would have been drowned.

They ran across the kitchen shouting angrily. Anne followed them with the trolley. This way and that, they ran. But the trolley was good at turning this way and that, too. Anne pushed with her foot, and pushed. Whenever the heroes tried to run to one side of the tray, she leaned over and jabbed at them with the umbrella to keep them in front of the tray. Spike's spike tinked against the tray. Enna carved a few bits off the umbrella.

But it did no good. Within minutes, Anne had pushed and prodded and herded them up against the back door where the cat flap was. She let them hack at the tray, while she leaned over and pushed the cat flap open with the umbrella.

"There's a way out!" squeaked Marlene.

"Stupid! It's just tempting us!" shouted Enna.

But Anne gave the heroes no choice. She held the cat flap open and shoved hard with her foot. The tray went right up against the door. The heroes were forced to leap out through the cat flap or be squashed.

"We'll get in another way!" Enna Hittims shouted angrily as the flap banged shut.

"No, you won't!" said Anne. She left the trolley pushed up against the door, and she turned the kitchen table over and pushed that up against the back of the trolley to keep it where it was.

Chapter 8
The End

She was just setting off to make sure all the windows were shut when she heard a car outside. It had to be her dad. She knew the growly sound of his car as he turned it around in the road before he backed down into the garage. Anne looked quickly up at the kitchen clock. He was back almost two hours early.

"I can't let them stab his eyes!" she gasped. She raced across the hall. In her head she saw the heroes standing on the garden wall and climbing up Mr Smith as he walked back from the garage. She had to warn him before he got out of the car.

She dragged the front door open and made warning signs with the umbrella.

Mr Smith smiled at her from the car. The car was already swinging round backward into the driveway. Anne stood where she was, with the umbrella up. She held her breath. The heroes were standing about half-way up the drive. Marlene was pointing at the car and gasping as always. "Another monster!"

"Go for its big black feet!" Enna shouted, and she led the three heroes at a run towards the car.

Mr Smith never saw them. He backed the car briskly down the drive. Half-way there, the heroes saw the danger. Marlene screamed, and they all turned and ran.

But the car, even slowing down, was moving faster than they could run. Anne watched the big, black, zig-zag tyre roll over the top of them. There was the tiniest little crunch. Much as she hated the heroes by now, Anne let her breath out with a shudder. Before Anne could lower the umbrella, there was a sharp hiss. The magic sword, and perhaps the magic spike, too, could still do damage. Mr Smith jumped out of the car. Anne ran across the lawn, and they both watched the right-hand back tyre sink into flat squashiness.

Mr Smith looked sadly from the tyre to Anne's face. "Your face has gone down, too," he said. "Did you know?"

"Has it?" Anne put her hand up to feel. The mumps were now only two small lumps on both sides of her chin.

While she was feeling them, her father turned and got something out of the car. "Here you are," he said. He passed her a fat new drawing book and a large pack of felt tips. "I knew you were going to run out of drawing things today."

Anne looked at the rows of different colours and the thick book of paper. She knew her father hated going to the drawing shop. There was never anywhere to park, and he always got a parking ticket. But he had gone there specially and then come home early to give them to her.

"Thanks!" she said. "Er – I'm afraid there's rather a mess indoors."

Mr Smith smiled. "Then isn't it lucky you're so much better?" he said. "You can tidy up while I'm putting the spare wheel on."

That seemed fair, Anne thought. She turned towards the house, thinking about where to start. The macaroni, the china lamp, or the milk? She looked down at the pack of felt tips while she tried to decide. They were a different make from the old lot. That was a good thing. She was almost sure that it was her drawings that had brought Enna Hittims and her friends to life like that. The old felt tips would not have been called Magic Markers for nothing.

Barrington Stoke would like to thank all its readers for commenting on the manuscript before publication and in particular:

Abbie Birch
Jessica Bladen
Louise Burgess
Jonathan Clewes
Shirley Davids
James Dickinson
Erin Donnelly
Nicole Dornin
Bryan Douglas
Bethany Eastwood
Lynn Fallaize
Lucy Ferguson
Dorothy Finan
Bethan Francis
George Gill
Harry Hartley
Emma Higgins
George Hubble
Josh
Gabby Lewis
Gail MacLeod
Euan Magurran
Claire McParland
Katie McTeir

Joe Moore
Craig Owen
Billie Page
Alex Palmer
Laura Parkes
Stephen Parsons
Amy Paxford
Harry Reynoldson
Adam Robinson
Jessica Rowley
Zak Saint
Emma Scott
Keira Silk
Scott Simpson
Vanessa Stead
David Stewart
Louis Still
Hannah Thompson
Francesca Webber
Paige Whitaker
Michael Whittet
Jacob Wilkinson
Stephanie Woodcock
Mathew Wormald

Become a Consultant!

Would you like to give us feedback on our titles before they are published? Contact us at the email address below – we'd love to hear from you!

info@barringtonstoke.co.uk
www.barringtonstoke.co.uk

More exciting new titles ...

Dragon!
by
Hilary McKay

When Max won't tidy his room, his witchy Aunt flies off in a temper – on her broomstick! Max is left on his own, with a dragon's egg to look after. But now the dragon's coming out ... and it's hungry!

You can order *Dragon!* directly from our website at:
www.barringtonstoke.co.uk.

King John

and the Abbot

by

Jan Mark

King John – Rich but greedy. He has all of England.

The Abbot – Rich but rude. He has a problem.

The Shepherd – Poor, but clever. He has nothing at all (except a scruffy dog).

King John has given the Abbot 3 puzzles. If the Abbot gets them wrong, King John will cut off his head! Can Jack save the Abbot's neck?

You can order *King John and the Abbot* directly from our website at: **www.barringtonstoke.co.uk**

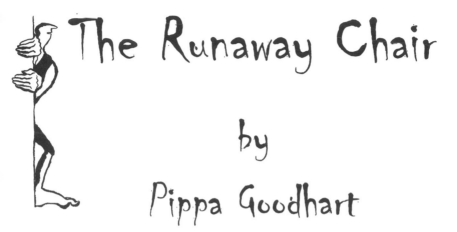

The Runaway Chair

by

Pippa Goodhart

When Aman's parents move house, they take the house with them! All that's left is a hole in the ground and an old chair called Shoddy. So Aman runs away ... and Shoddy comes with him! Can Shoddy help Aman find his way home?

You can order *The Runaway Chair* directly from our website at: **www.barringtonstoke.co.uk**